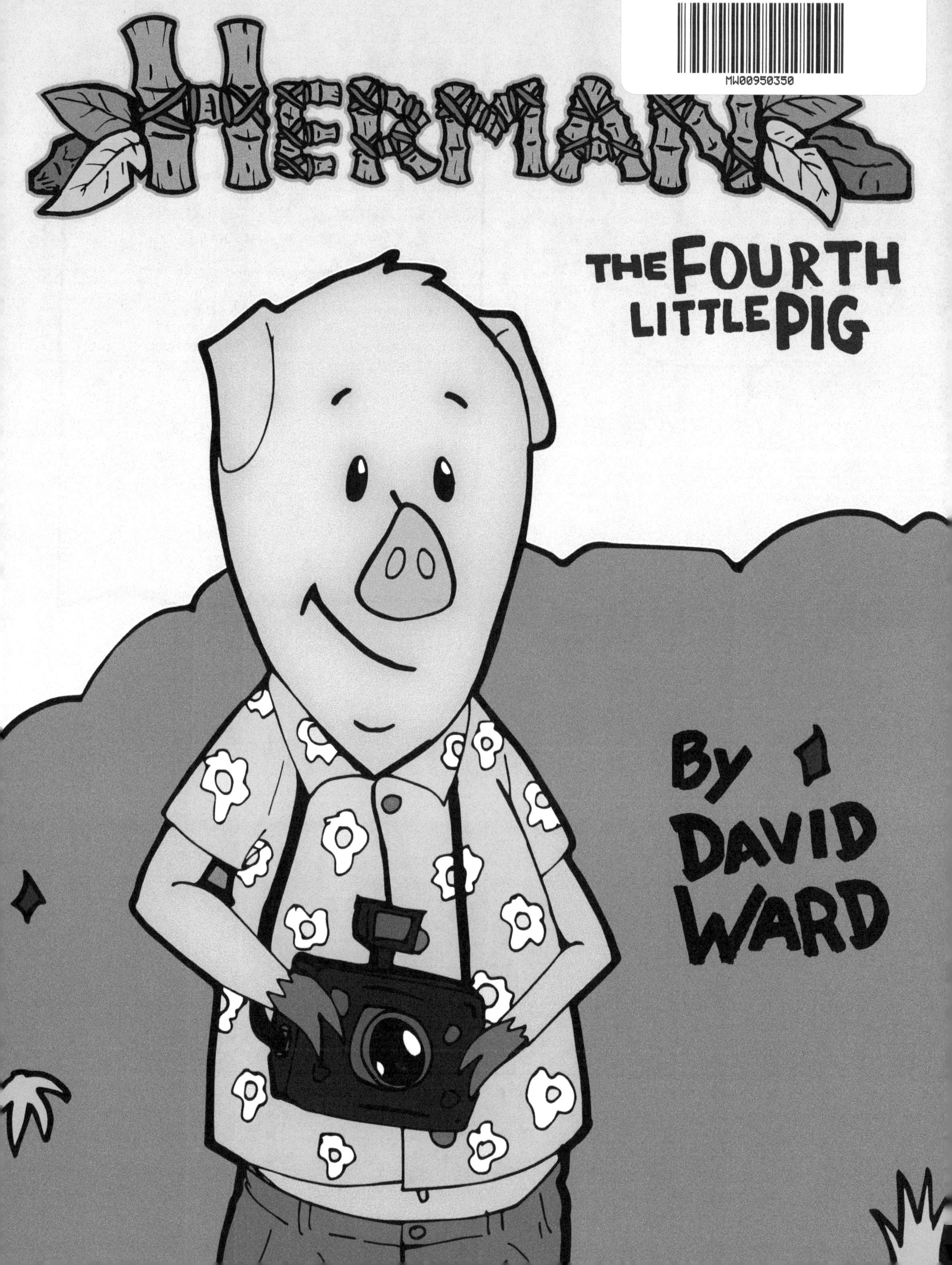
HERMAN
THE FOURTH LITTLE PIG
By DAVID WARD

ISBN 13: 978-1-64446-014-6

Illustrated by author.

1 2 3 4 5 6 7

Printed in the United States of America
Published by

R
Rowe Publishing
www.rowepub.com

For Josie,
who loves her piggies so

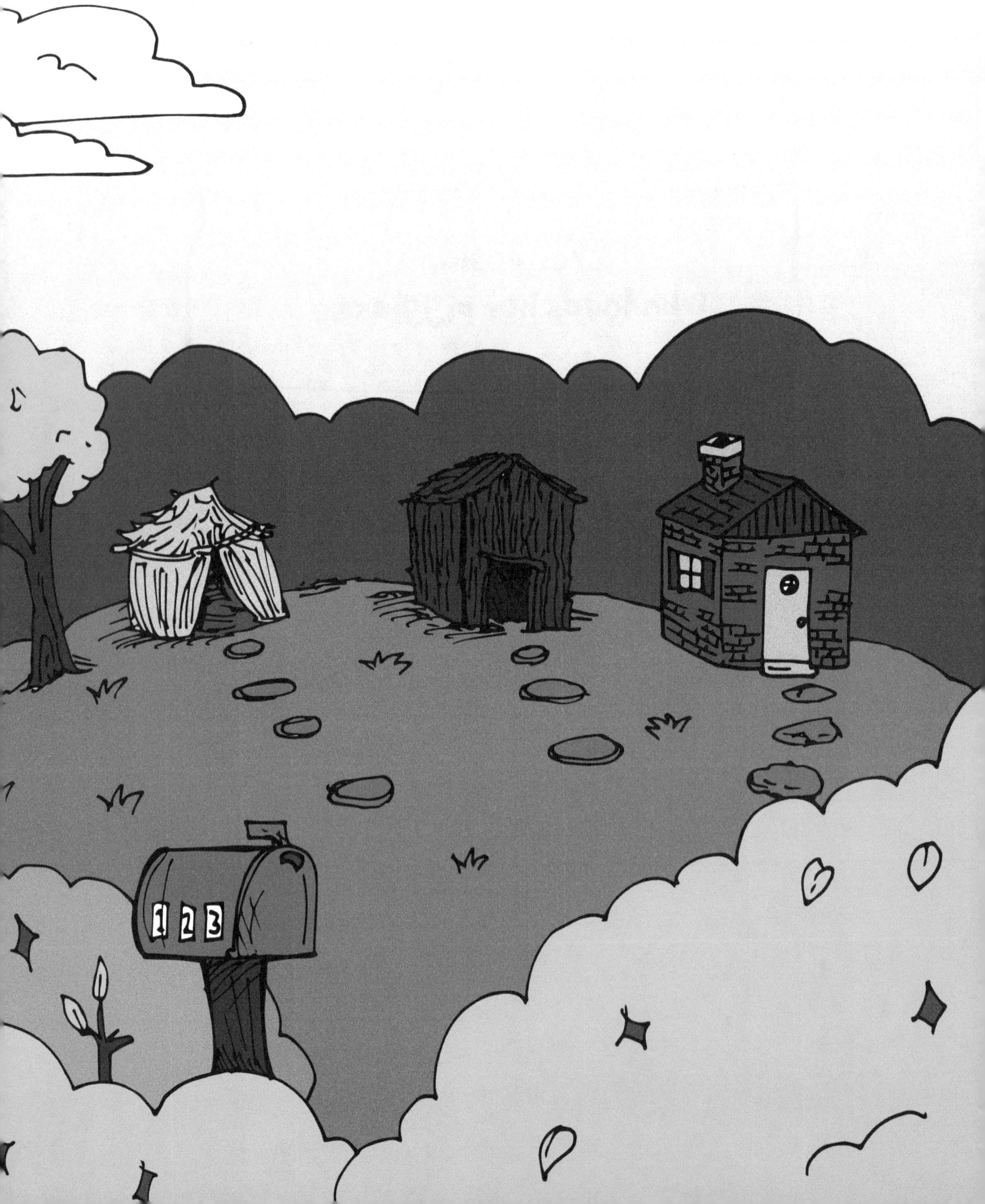
1 2 3

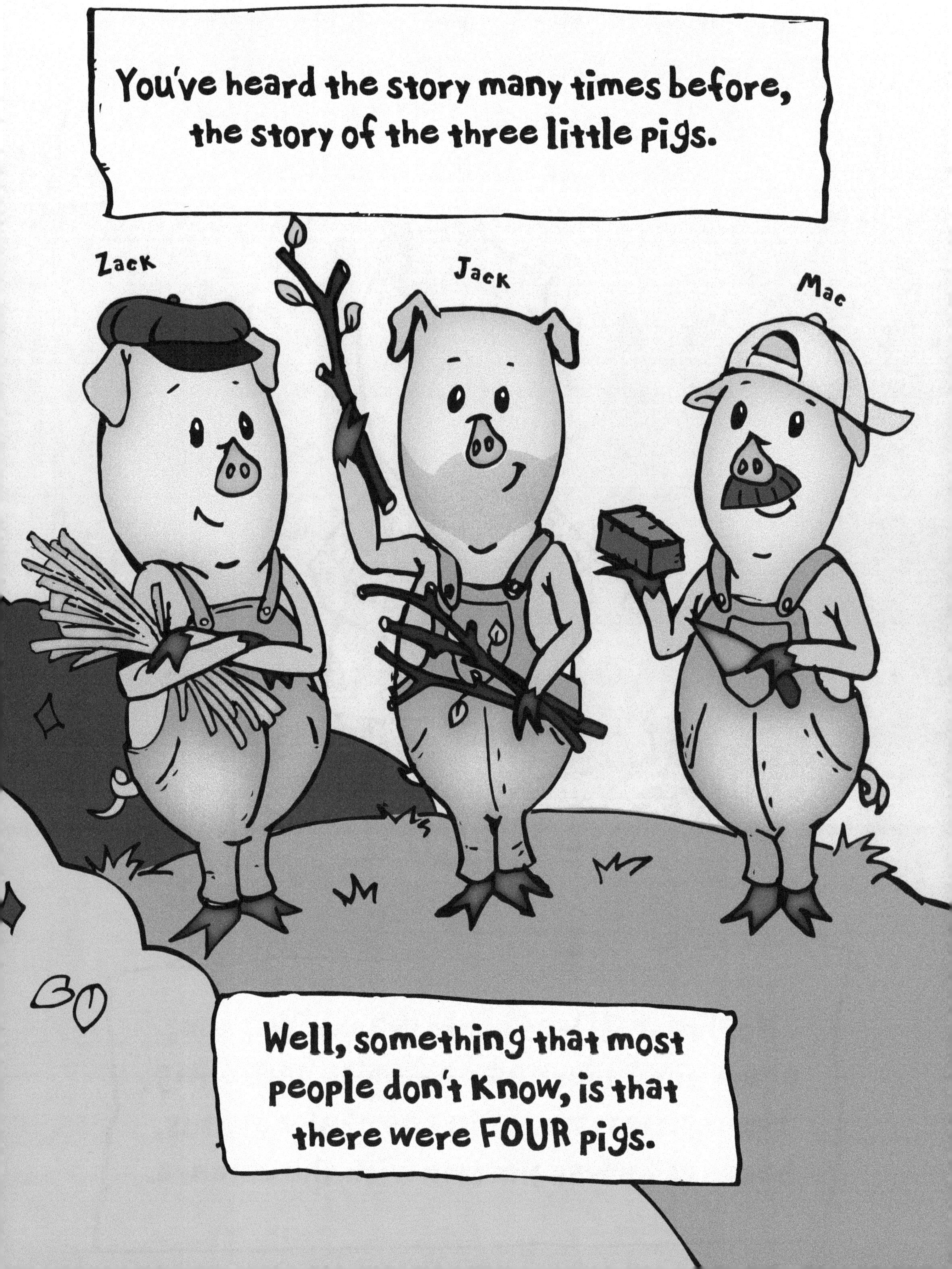
You've heard the story many times before, the story of the three little pigs.
Zack
Jack
Mac
Well, something that most people don't know, is that there were FOUR pigs.

Meet Herman, the fourth pig. Herman, much like his three brothers, was a pig with a skill. His skill wasn't about building a house with straw, or sticks, or bricks.

No, his skill was photography. You see, every time there was a family gathering, Herman was never in any of the photos, because he was the one with the camera.

Well, when the infamous day came that the ol' Big Bad Wolf blew down all those houses, Herman just happened to be on one of his daily nature hikes through the woods. He saw what that old wolf was doing, and, confident his brothers could take care of themselves, he felt it was best if he avoided the situation altogether.

So he ran. And he ran, and he ran. He ran as fast as he could through the woods, as fast as his little piggy legs could carry him.

He ran so far, that eventually, he made it to the ocean. He saw a nice little sailboat that no one seemed to be using, and he jumped right into that boat, and set sail for the open seas.

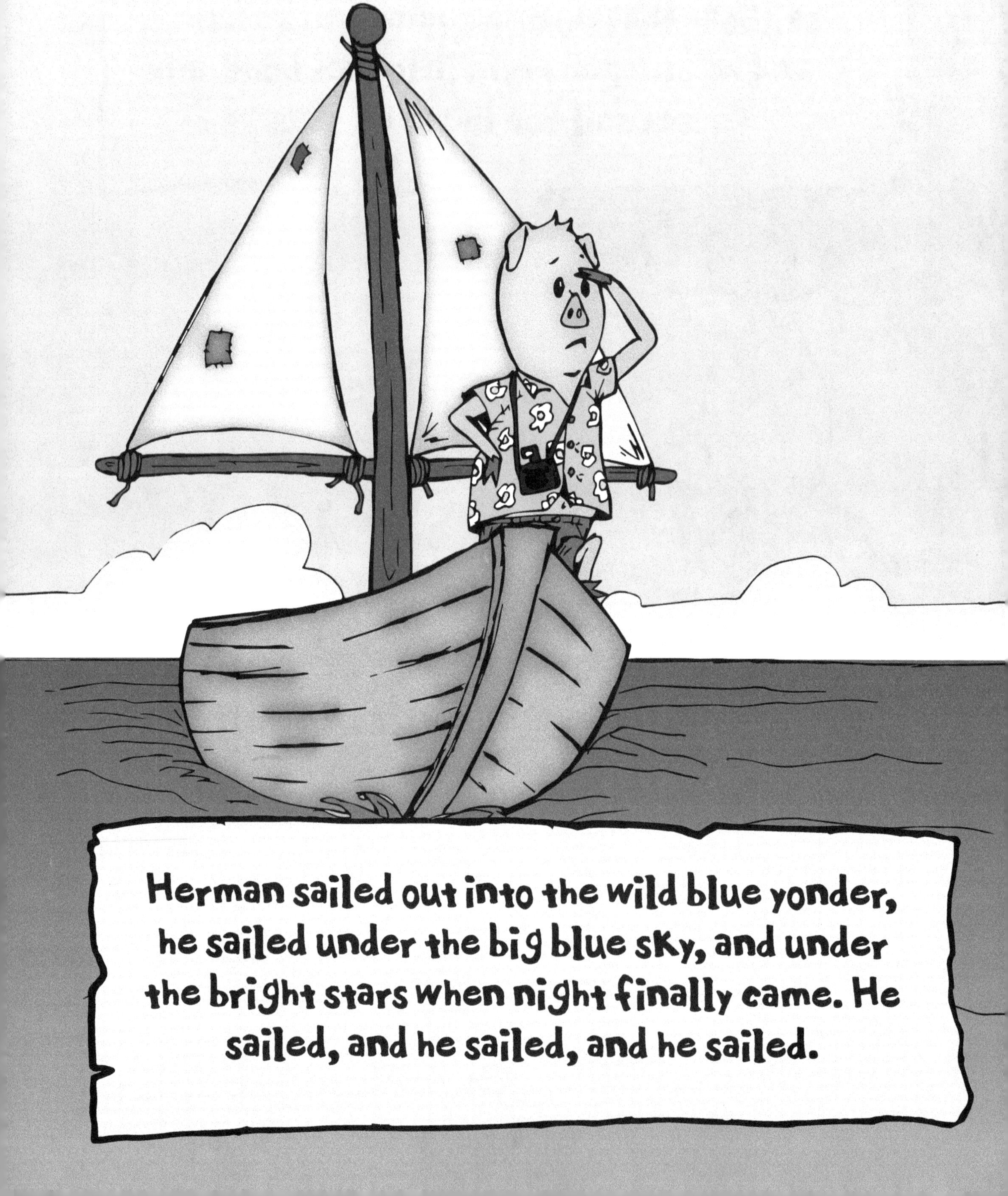

Herman sailed out into the wild blue yonder, he sailed under the big blue sky, and under the bright stars when night finally came. He sailed, and he sailed, and he sailed.

Herman was getting pretty tired of sailing,
when finally, he saw land again.

What do you think that land was?

Why, a beautiful tropical island!

After he landed on the island and tied his boat up all nice and neat, he surveyed his surroundings. He was going to need a shelter before night time. That's when he noticed that the palm trees had some nice big leaves. Those would make a great shelter!

Dusting his hands off, Herman stood proudly outside his little palm leaf shelter that he had spent all afternoon building. This would shield him from the hot sun in the daytime, and if it rained, he'd have something to keep him nice and dry.

And rain it did. It rained, and rained, and rained. And that rain got so heavy, it turned into a STORM.

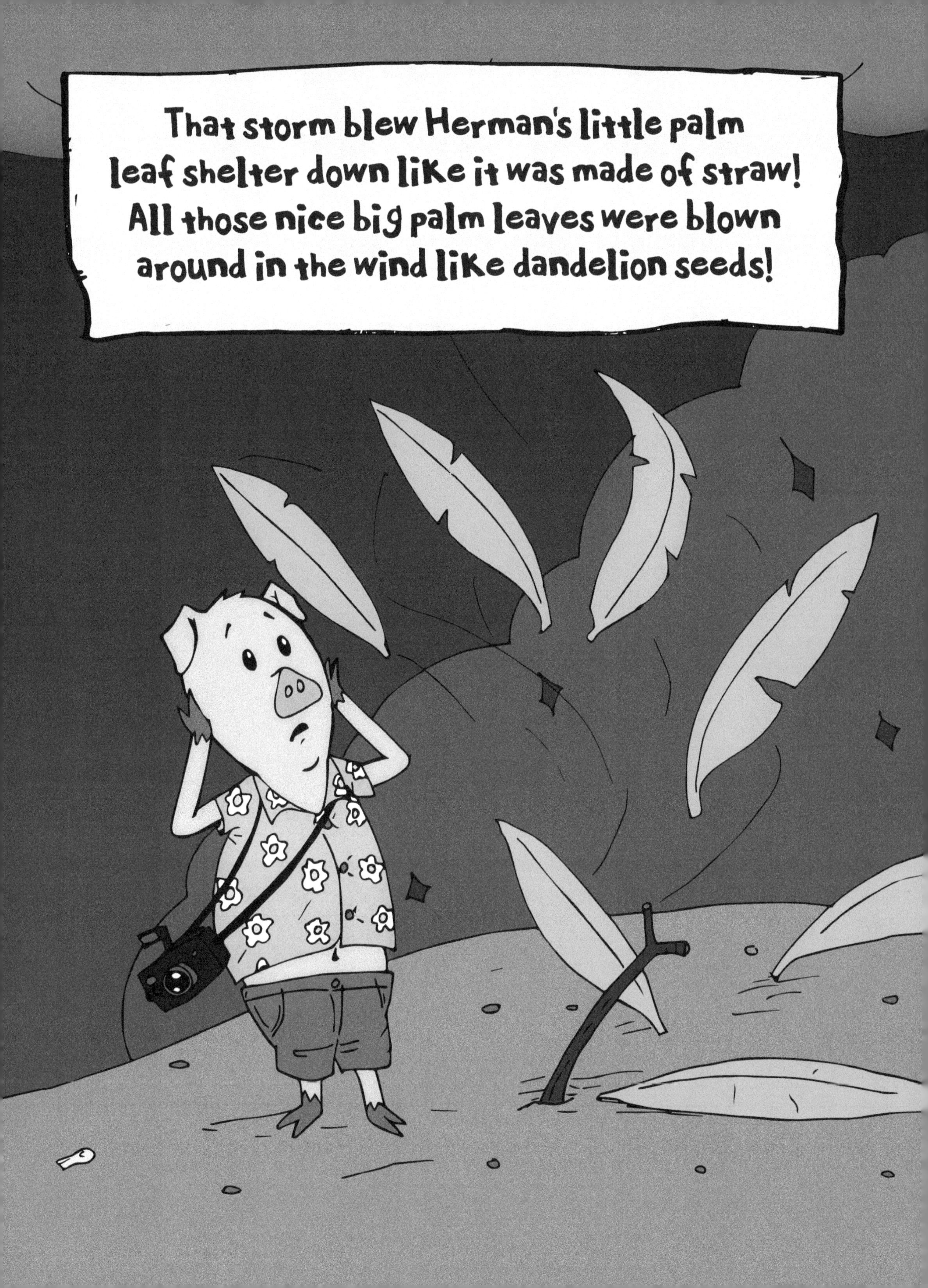
That storm blew Herman's little palm leaf shelter down like it was made of straw! All those nice big palm leaves were blown around in the wind like dandelion seeds!

Herman didn't know what to do. He sat sadly in the pouring rain, getting wet, cold, muddy, and his sinuses were acting up to boot.

The next morning, the sun came out and dried everything up. Herman was ecstatic to be nice and dry and warm (and his sinuses were also doing much better, thank you for asking). He decided to resume his daily hikes, and went on a little stroll through the island jungle.

As he walked through the jungle, he saw another type of tropical plant that would make a good shelter too! This time, he'd build one out of bamboo! This would be much more sturdy than those silly palm tree leaves. Why, he could build a little house out of this!

Herman got to work getting his bamboo polls all situated. He got a lot of them together, and tied them with little bits of vine he had also found in the jungle. It was a very long and tedious process, but he kept at it all day long.

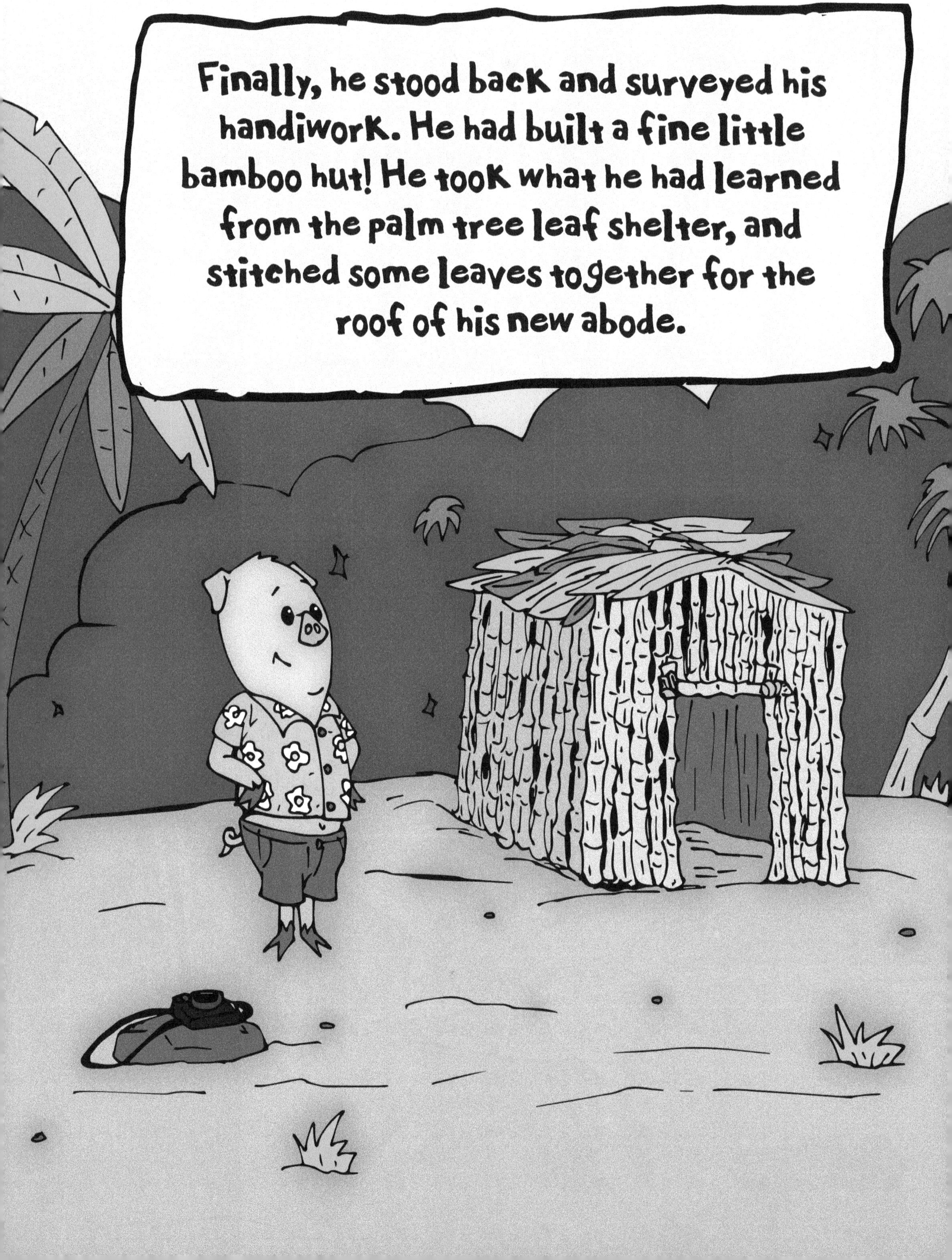
Finally, he stood back and surveyed his handiwork. He had built a fine little bamboo hut! He took what he had learned from the palm tree leaf shelter, and stitched some leaves together for the roof of his new abode.

Herman was enjoying himself immensely now; doing something so productive encouraged him to build something else, so he fashioned himself a little ukulele and played some music as he sat by his campfire that night.

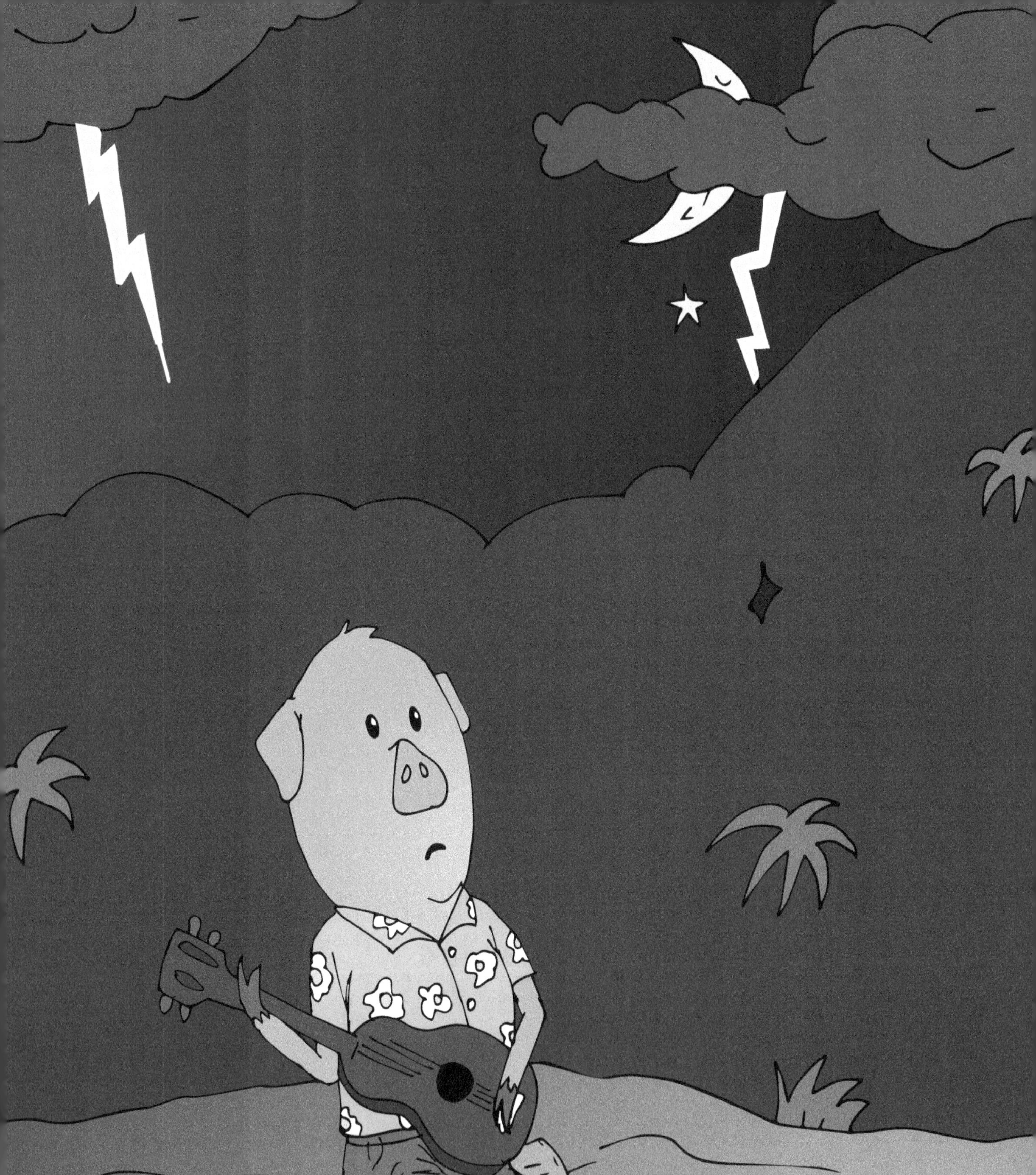

But his joy was to be short-lived; unfortunately, two nights later, ANOTHER big storm blew through, and again, destroyed his shelter.

Herman was distraught. He had worked so hard on his bamboo hut! It wasn't anywhere NEAR as flimsy as that palm tree leaf shelter he had thrown together. This one was supposed to last a long time! But the stormy winds were too strong, and it blew his little house down.

Finally, the rain stopped for a little while, and Herman trudged sadly through the jungle. He was depressed and exhausted. Nothing he did seemed to work.

The rain started up again, just a light drizzle this time, fortunately. The best shelter Herman could find was a coconut tree. It didn't offer much protection from the falling water, but at least it was better than nothing at all.

The coconut tree might have offered a tiny bit of protection from the falling rain, but it didn't offer any protection from falling COCONUTS. A coconut broke loose from the tree, and fell down, bonking Herman right on the head.

But that coconut knocked some sense into Herman, it snapped him out of his sad thoughts. He could find a better shelter! He knew it! He couldn't give up now, no sir! He was on a tropical island, living the dream! He'd make it work one way or another!

This new-found motivation inspired him to get up off his duff and take another hike! Hikes were always good for thinking!

Herman hiked across the island and began climbing the little island mountain. He climbed high up the mountainside, and looked around to see what he could see.

Peering into the distance, Herman saw something that piqued his curiosity.

Was that a CAVE???

Herman made his way over to the cave, and peered inside. It looked empty, and Herman didn't see any signs that anyone (or anyTHING) lived in it. Perhaps this would work as a shelter!

Herman went into the cave and looked around. It was dry, and cool from the hot sun. Plus, it was big enough to stretch his legs. Yes, this would work. This would work quite nicely!

Outside, that old rain started falling again, and Herman could hear the thunder rolling, and see the lightning flashing. This storm was even bigger and badder than the last one!

But this time, Herman didn't mind. He actually liked the sound of the storm, because THIS time, he was nice and dry in his new shelter. He warmed his hands by his cozy little fire.

He slept very soundly that night; he had built a nice bed out of bamboo and palm tree leaves, and it was super comfortable. The rain raged outside, but it wasn't anywhere near as loud as Herman's snoring.

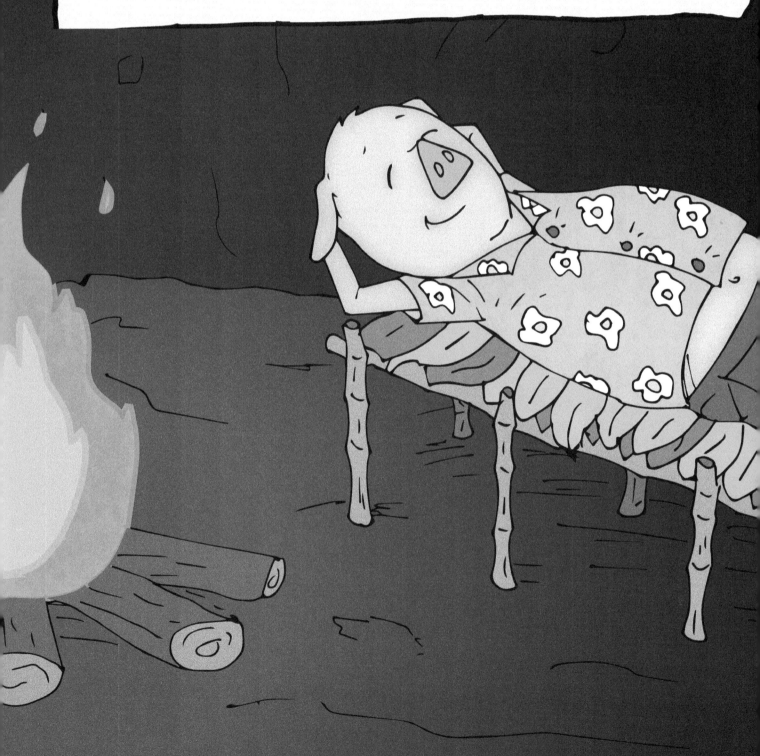

The next day, Herman stepped out onto his new front porch, sipping some delicious coffee (where he got coffee, I'll never know). He had a pretty nice view from his new home, so he grabbed his camera, and snapped a beautiful photograph. It was such a lovely picture, he decided to use it for a postcard.

Wish You Were Here!

Love,
Herman

3 Little Pigs
123 Brick House Rd.
Swinesburgh Village

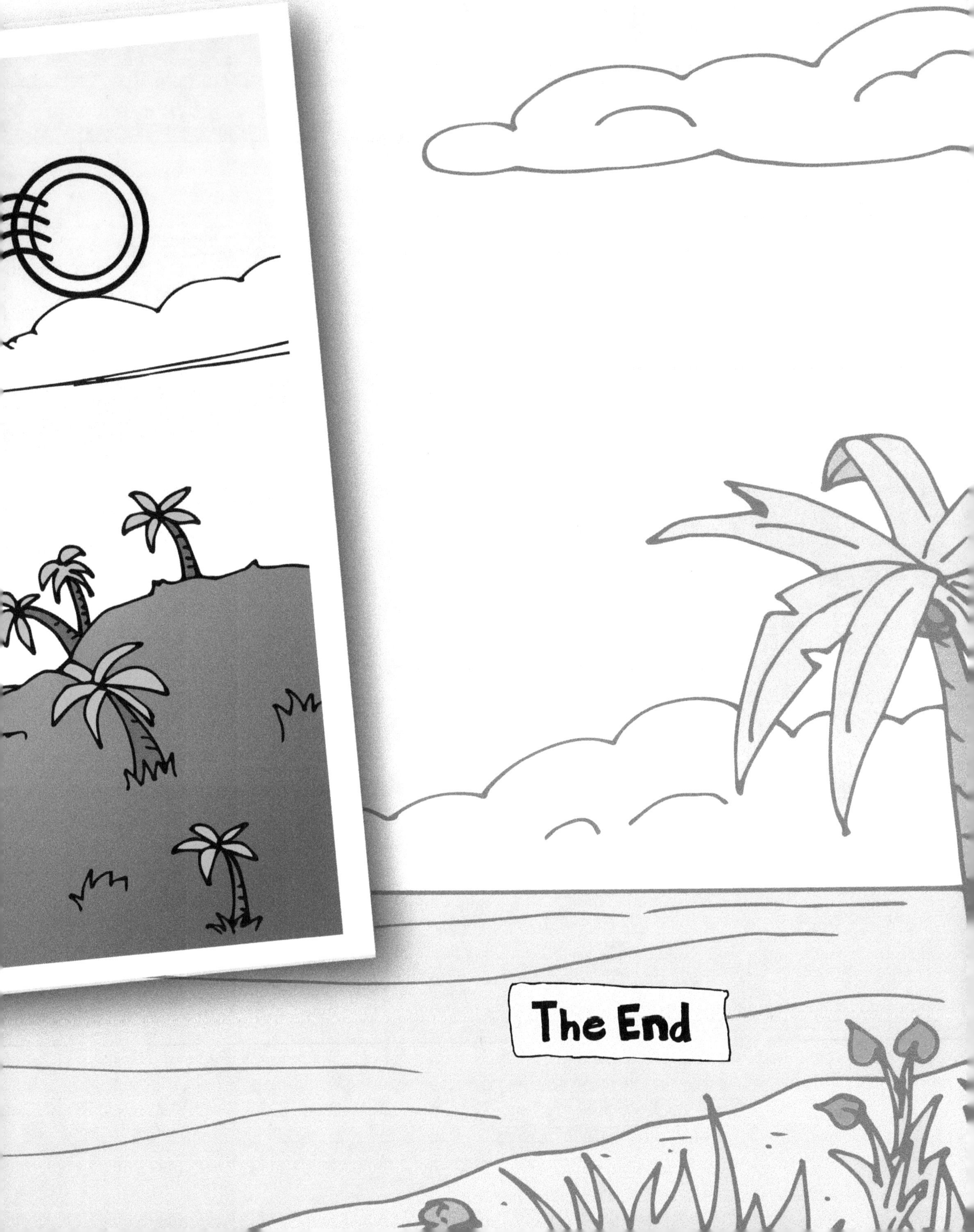
The End

CPSIA information can be obtained
at www.ICGtesting.com
Printed in the USA
JSHW040033210622
27186JS00004B/121